This book belongs to:

____

____

Eva's Unselfish Love

Title: Eva's Unselfish Love

Written by: Mridula Mitra Vyas

Published by: Maple Publishers
1 Brunel Way, Slough,
SL1 1FQ, UK

First Published: January 2021

ISBN: 978-1-914366-02-4

Copyright © Mridula Mitra Vyas

Edited by: Hemlata Iyer

Illustrated by: Abjini Chattopadhay / White Magic Studios

Designed by: White Magic Studios

Eva's Unselfish Love

Written by

Mridula Mitra Vyas

Illustrated by

Abjini Chattopadhay

Princess Ballerina Fairy Eva, as she likes to call herself, lives in a beautiful country in Central America called Costa Rica. She lives with her parents, her big brother, her little brother and her grandmother. They live in a lovely cottage on a green valley called the Arenal Volcano.

Every morning, as Eva opens her eyes and looks out the window, she can see a huge volcano mountain kissing the blue sky. That mountain has a story of its own.

Long, long ago on a Monday, on July 29, 1968 at 7:30 in the morning, suddenly the mountain begins to rumble. Soon after the ground under the mountain starts to shake. Then like a thousand angry dragons, it begins to spit fire. Until heaps of hot lava, rocks and ash pile up over a large area. This continues for days and nights. That scares the villagers around the mountain. They begin to run far, far away from it. But not everyone can escape. Before the volcano stops erupting rocks, lava and ash, it kills eighty seven people and burns three beautiful villages.

Today the mountain is calm and quiet. The valley around the mountain is green. It is trimmed with palm trees and filled with shrubs and bushes of pink, orange and red flowers. Behind the valley lies the coffee plantation. As we know, Costa Rica is known for its coffee. Along the coffee plantation stand rows of tall trees with golden yellow flowers called Cortez Amarillo. Some like to call it Golden Shower Tree.

Costa Rica is famous for its beautiful rainforests and cloud forests. Every year during the dry season thousands of visitors visit the rainforests and the cloud forests of Costa Rica. One Saturday morning, Eva and her family visit the Cano Negro rainforest.

Along the rainforest runs the Rio Frio which means Cold River. While Eva and her family sail along the bank of the river which lies on the border of Nicaragua, they enjoy many interesting sights and scenes.

First, they see a bed (group) of **sloths** hanging upside down from a big fig tree. It makes Eva and her brothers very curious. They cannot take their eyes off them.

Next, they notice a colony (group) of **tiny bats** clinging on to a branch of a tree. Eva learns from her big brother that bats are <u>nocturnal</u>. It means they are awake and active at night and sleep during the day. But most animals and human beings are <u>diurnal</u>. It means they are awake and active during the day and sleep at night.

Then they see a barrel (group) of **white-faced monkeys** playing amongst themselves. Eva and her brothers find the little ones so naughty and so cute that they just cannot take their eyes off them.

That is when they spot a **Green Iguana** on a tree. It is known to be **arboreal**. That means it loves to hang on trees. To Eva, a rainforest is like a wonderland. It is so colorful with buds, blooms, and blossoms that grow on trees, shrubs, plants, and vines. There are so many birds of all different shapes, sizes and colors perched on the tree tops. Some of them hide behind the leaves and sing, others chirp, and some others love to whistle.

As they look around, they catch sight of a **Caiman** sunbathing at the edge of the river along the rainforest. They watch it from far until it takes a dive into the river and disappears.

While they are having a good time, Eva decides, when she grows up, she wants to spend all her time in the rainforests and learn about the trees, the plants, the flowers, the animals, the birds, and the butterflies that live there.

Just then they see a cartload (group) of **Geoffroy's Spider Monkeys**. Their long limbs and their long tails make them look like spiders. They usually move around in a group of ten to forty of them. Later they learn from their mama that they are among the largest and the most intelligent monkeys in America.

There are only two seasons in Costa Rica, the dry season and the rainy season. In Costa Rica weather can be shifty. It can be from sunny to foggy, misty, cloudy and rainy, all in one day.

One Sunday morning as Eva wakes up, she looks out the window and guess what? She finds something missing! It feels so strange! She quietly steps out, but the air feels misty. She walks in, rubs her eyes, and tries to see it again from her window. But it's not there!

"The Giant Mountain is Missing!!!" She whispers.

It seems as if the mountain is totally wiped out from the sky.

But how can that be? Where can it go? Eva is afraid something is wrong with her eyes. She goes back to bed and keeps thinking about it until she falls

asleep. Then suddenly she hears her father's voice. "Eva wake up, wake up, dear. The sun is up."

Eva wakes up and quickly runs to the window.

"The Giant Mountain is Back!!!" She screams with joy.

"It was always there dear," says her father. "It's just that we couldn't see it this morning."

"Why, why couldn't we see it, dada?"

"We couldn't see it because it was hiding behind the mist. Since the mist lifted, we can see it again. Are you happy now?"

"Yes dada, I am very happy now."

Later that afternoon as Eva walks along the garden path, she hears a squeaky sound around a bush. She bends down, looks through the leaves and finds a beautiful bird.

"How did you get there dear?" Eva whispers.

"I fell down," the bird twitters. "Are you hurting dear?"

"Yes, I am."

"What is your name?" Eva asks.

"I am Polly."

"I am Eva. Can I help you Polly?"

"Yes, you may." Polly twitters.

Eva gently picks up Polly from the bush and asks her.

"How did you fall into the bush dear?"

"Well, it's a long story. I left home early this morning. But I was caught in a storm. I couldn't fight against the wind. It kept pushing me. So I kept gliding with the wind. Until I got so far away from home, I knew I was lost. Yet I didn't give up. I kept trying to find my way home. But after a while I was so tired, I must have fainted. The next thing I knew, I had fallen into a bush and couldn't move any more. That's when I knew I had bruised my wings too."

"Polly, I am so sorry you are lost and hurt. Where are you from? I never saw a bird so beautiful like you."

"Thank you dear, I am a Scarlet macaw. My home is in Jaco along the Pacific coast. I belong to the parrot family."

Eva asks Polly to wait there while she runs back to the cottage to call her father.

"Dada come look who I found in the bush!" Eva sounds excited.

"Who did you find dear?" Eva's father asks her while Eva walks him towards the bush.

"Come, come. Look! Her name is Polly. Isn't she beautiful?"

Eva's father takes one look at Polly and says. "Yes dear, she is beautiful!"

"Dada, can we keep her with us? She is hurt and lost.

A strong wind blew her far, far away from her home."

"Yes dear but we have to first ask Polly to see what she wants to do," says her father.

"Ok, Polly do you want to live with us? I will take good care of you, I promise," says Eva.

"You are so kind, my dear Eva. But are you sure you won't get tired of me? Macaws can be very loud and noisy at times."

"Oh! No! No! I love birds. You will be my best friend."

"And so are you my friend Eva," says Polly.

"A friend in need is a friend indeed. Today you promised to take care of me and made me your best friend. I will always remember this day, Eva."

"Thank you Polly," says Eva and asks her what she would like to eat.

"I love seeds, fruits, flowers, leaves, palm nuts, figs, nectar and sometimes I even crave for clay from the river bank. Isn't it strange?"

"Well, I am sure if I were a macaw, I would love it too," says Eva.

Later that day Eva is happy to see her father bring home a bird's stand for Polly, and not a cage. Eva's father knew that Eva would not want to keep her best friend in a cage. That would make her sad. That makes both Eva and Polly very happy. Polly enjoys talking and mimicking all day long and goes to her bird's stand at night after everyone goes to bed. Each day Polly begins to feel better than the day before. But every now and again when Polly remembers her home in Jaco, she looks sad. That is when Eva dresses up as a princess, or a ballerina, or a fairy and sings and dances and makes merry. Watching Eva sing and dance makes Polly forget her sorrows, but only for a while. Once Eva asks her.

"Polly, tell me, what makes you really happy?"

"Only if I can go home once," Polly says.

"What if you don't come back?"

"Of course I will come back and see you again. You must know that macaws are very loyal to their friends. I will come back, I promise."

"Will you really? What if you can't find your way back?" Eva asks.

"If I can find my way home, then I know I will find my way back." Polly replies.

But Eva is not happy. She talks to her grandmother whom she loves very much. At first her grandmother quietly listens to her. Then she tells her.

"My dear Eva, tell me do you really love Polly?"

"Yes, thama (that's what she calls her grandmother) I really love her. She is my best friend."

"Then you must do what makes her happy. If you really love her, then what makes her happy should make you happy too. Just like if she is sad, then won't that make you sad too?" Eva quietly thinks for a while. Then she asks. "But thama, what if she never comes back?"

"Well, if Polly tells you that she will come back, then you must believe her. If you love her, you must also TRUST her and set her FREE, so that she can be happy."

Eva quietly thinks for a while and then goes to Polly.

"I will let you out in the morning, Polly, so you can fly home and be happy," Eva tells her.

"Do you really mean that, Eva? You must know I will be back in a few days, I promise."

"I know you will, Polly. I trust you," says Eva.

That evening after Eva dresses up in her pink, shimmering dress, her silver crown studded with jewels and her satin, pink shoes, she plays the part of a Princess Ballerina Fairy Eva. Polly enjoys watching Eva perform. Then Eva gives Polly a kiss, wishes her good night and goes to bed.

The next morning Eva wakes up early, goes to Polly, gives her a kiss and lets her out. Polly perches on her shoulder for a moment, kisses her goodbye and takes to her wings as she twitters.

"I will see you soon, Eva."

Eva waves at her as she sees the morning sun glittering on a pair of red, yellow and blue wings in flight.

Eva misses Polly. She counts her days and nights waiting for Polly to return. Then one morning while Eva is sleeping, she hears a voice calling out her name.

"Rise and shine my dear Eva. Polly is back."

Eva wakes up, looks around, and finds Polly perched on the windowsill.

"Polly!!! Is that really you or am I dreaming?"

She screams with joy. Eva cannot believe her eyes.

"You are not dreaming, dear." Polly says.

"I told you I would be back. I kept my promise and look who I brought with me. My friend Tutu, she is a Keel Billed toucan."

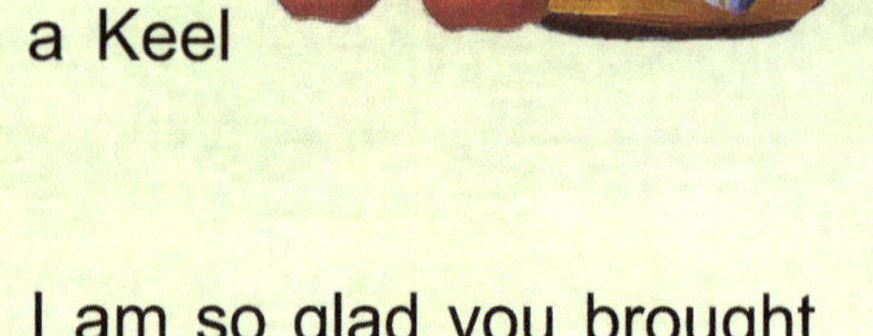

"Hello, Tutu. Nice to see you both! Polly, I am so glad you brought your friend," says Eva.

"Although most birds like to be friends with their own kind, I am a bit different," says Polly. "I like to make friends with any and every kind of bird I meet."

"You are very special Polly and so is your friend. What does Tutu love to eat?" Eva asks.

"Well toucans love fruits, insects, small reptiles and believe it or not also the eggs of other birds," says Tutu. Eva treats Tutu and Polly to a bowl of fruits. Then Tutu asks her.

"What do you love to eat Eva?"

"I love pizza, hot dogs, French fries, chicken nuggets, French toasts, fried eggs with rice and butter, donuts, ice cream, chocolate cake, banana chips, smoothies, strawberries and raspberries."

Then Eva asks Tutu. "Do you enjoy flying?"

"No, not really", says Tutu.

"Toucans are not known for flying too high or too far" says Polly. Then Eva looks at Polly and says. "Polly, I know you love to fly, don't you?"

"Yes, we macaws love to fly far, far away."

Eva thinks for a while and then she says. "Well, though we don't have wings like you do, we fly too you know."

"Are you talking about those loud, shiny, giant birds with big shiny wings flying high up in the sky?" Polly asks.

"Yes, it is called airplane," says Eva, "it takes us far away from one country to another. Sometimes it flies over oceans and mountains too. My dada says a long, long time ago there were two brothers. They dreamed of flying. Then one day they came up with the idea of building an airplane. Now we all fly."

"Really!!! Do you know their names?" Toucan asks.

"Yes, they are Orville and Wilbur. But people call them Wright brothers. When I grow up I'll read more about them and get to know everything about airplanes."

"Good for you, Eva! We macaws are known to be smart too you know. But wish we could read and write too."

"That would be so much fun, Polly!" Eva says.

"Yes, I think so too!" Then Polly looks around and says. "We have to leave now so we can get home before the sun goes down."

"I hope you will be back soon, Polly," says Eva.

"Yes Eva, you know I will be back again soon."

Polly and Tutu take off on their long flight, as Eva waves them goodbye.

Days and nights go by while Eva waits for Polly. Then one morning Eva wakes up as she hears that friendly voice.

"Rise and shine my dear Eva. Polly is back."

Eva opens her eyes and sees Polly perched on her window with another tiny little bird next to her.

"Polly! I am so happy to see you. I see you brought a pretty little friend with you. What is her name?"

"She is a Ruby-throated hummingbird. Her name is Hala. She is an amazing bird," says Polly.

"Really! Tell me all about her," Eva sounds excited.

"Well, Hala lives on nectar. But she eats tree sap and insects too. She is also very quick and smart."

"What else? Tell me more about her," says Eva.

1. "Well… she flies 30 miles in one hour!"

2. "She flaps her wings 70 times in a second!"

3. "She sees colors that even humans cannot see!"

4. "She weighs 3 grams and eats 43 grams of sugar daily!"

5. "She flies 18 to 20 hours without any break!"

6. "Once she visits a flower, she never forgets it!!"

7. "She moves 3000 miles away every year!"

8. "And guess what! Like an acrobat she can fly forward, backward and upside down!!"

"Oh! My Goodness!! I am so happy to learn all about hummingbirds," says Eva. "Hala! I only wish I could be like you. I know all my friends too would want to be like you. You are so special!"

"Yes! Hala is special," says Poly. "But I also know we have something special in all of us and by that I mean in everyone of us. Don't you think so?"

"Yes, I agree," says Hala.

"But I don't see anything special in me," says Eva.

"Eva, you are so kind and loving to everyone and that makes you very special," says Polly.

"Thank you Polly. Hala, do you want to visit the flowers in our valley and enjoy the sweet nectar?"

"Sure, thank you Eva. I'll be back soon." So Hala whisks away into the valley and begins to sip the nectar from the flowers. That is when Eva treats Polly with some seeds, palm nuts and figs. Before the sun goes down, Hala returns. Then Polly and Hala say goodbye to Eva and fly away to their home in the rainforest.

But Polly always comes back to Eva and they spend time together. Until one day Polly tells Eva that she is tired of flying back and forth. She would rather live with Eva for the rest of her life, if it is ok with her and her family. It makes Eva so happy that she runs from one room to another and gathers everyone around Polly and says.

"Listen everyone I am so happy to say that from today my best friend Polly will live with us forever and ever!!!"

Seeing Eva so happy, everyone thanks Polly and welcomes her with a big smile. That evening after dinner Polly tells them all about her childhood days spent in a rainforest. Since that night, Eva, her big brother and her little brother always wait for Polly to tell them stories of the rainforests. Thus Polly becomes the most famous storyteller in Eva's family. Once Eva asks.

"Polly, how do you know so much about rainforests?"

"Eva dear, I was born in a rainforest and I grew up in a rainforest. We Scarlet macaws live our whole lives in a rainforest. We also live very long and we perch on a high branch of a tall tree and watch everything that goes on in the rainforest. We gawk at all the comings and goings of the animals and the birds all day long. We gaze at them while they are fighting, playing, hunting, or sun-bathing." Then Polly asks Eva and her brothers.

"Did you know, the rainforests keep our earth healthy?"

"No, we didn't know that." They all say it together.

"Let me tell you," says Polly. "All the trees and the plants in the rainforests breathe out or give out oxygen which we breathe in. Oxygen is good for you and me and all of us. It keeps us alive and healthy. But guess what? The trees and the plants breathe in or take in what we breathe out or give out which is called carbon dioxide. Can you say it? "

"Yes we can." They take turn and repeat the word: "Carbon dioxide."

"Wonderful! Did you know the rainforests bring rain?"

"I was going to ask you about it." Again, all three of them say it out loud together.

"Let me tell you," says Polly. "The leaves of the trees give out moisture which means water. When the sun is hot during the summer months, the water gets warm, turns into vapor and rises high up and forms into rainclouds. Then the rainclouds break into rain when the trees once again take in the moisture and the cycle goes on and on and on. Get it?"

"Yes we got it!" They all say it together.

"Now you can see without rainforests how unhealthy our earth would be."

After listening to Polly talk about the rainforests, Eva begins to dream of a day when she will grow up and visit all the rainforests of the world and learn everything about the trees, the flowers, the animals and the birds that live in the rainforests.

The End

3. Eva's Unselfish Love:

Q.1. Can you find out how many rainforests are there in all?

And where they are located?

Q.2. Do rainforests help in keeping the earth healthy?

If yes, can you explain how?

Q.3. Name the collective noun of the animals mentioned in the book.

Q.4. What is a **volcano**? And what happens when it erupts?

Q.5. Name the two brothers who dreamed of flying. Did their dreams come true and how?

Q.6. Where is **Costa Rica**?

Q.7. Did you enjoy reading the book? If yes or no explain why?

2. The Snowman and the Sunshine in Switzerland:

Q.1. What do the Swiss call their Santa Claus?

Q.2. In Switzerland who accompanies the Santa Claus every year on December 6?

Q.3. What is an Advent Window?

Q.4. Who is St. Nicholas?

Q.5. Name the dessert that cheered up Kai.

Q.6. Name the famous mountain range in Switzerland.

Q.7. Did you enjoy reading the book? If yes or no explain why.

1. Frogster Loudmouth's Tadpole Days:

Q.1. What does **amphibian** mean? Is there an **amphibian** in the story?

Q.2. What is **hibernation**? Name the animals that **hibernate**.

Q.3. Name all the **continents** mentioned in the story.

Q.4. Did you learn any new word in the book?

Q.5. What does Evolution mean? Can you explain?

Q.6. What are the different types of frogs and where do they live?

Q.7. Did you enjoy reading the book? If yes or no explain why.

Author: Mridula Mitra Vyas's **A Wounded Tigress** (a collection of novellas) was published in December 1996 which earned her an invitation to read her book at the Freer Gallery in the Smithsonian Institute in Washington, DC; the World Bank; George Mason University; Barnes & Noble; and Borders Bookshop.

Ms. Vyas began her career as a journalist in India. In February 1973 she left for USA to study journalism and never looked back. Later she worked as a Technical Writer in Washington, DC and made her home in Virginia. As a poet, playwright and a novelist, she pledges to donate 50% of the sale from her books to children in distress through UNICEF, UNHCR and Artists United against Childhood Hunger. **Frogster Loudmouth's Tadpole Days**, her first Children's book was published in February 2018.

Abjini Chattopadhaya is fourteen years old, born in Florida. She lives in Maryland with her parents. Abjini is an excellent classical singer, plays piano, violin, loves to paint, and aspires to be a scientist like both her parents.

BOOKS PUBLISHED

- A Wounded Tigress (A collection of six novellas)
- Frogster Loudmouth's Tadpole Days
- The Snowman and the Sunshine in Switzerland

BOOKS TO BE PUBLISHED SOON

Novels
- A Sacred Lust
- The Disillusion
- House of Shahibag

Children's books
- Actions Speak Louder
- Crystal's Dream
- Jabber in the Jungle
- Cyrus goes to Galapagos

www.ingramcontent.com/pod-product-compliance
Lightning Source LLC
Chambersburg PA
CBHW042133030726
47599CB00002B/456